Old Friends

LYNNE BARASCH

Frances Foster Books   Farrar, Straus and Giroux   New York

Copyright © 1998 by Lynne Barasch
All rights reserved
Distributed in Canada by Douglas & McIntyre Ltd.
Printed and bound in the United States of America by Worzalla
Typography by Caitlin Martin
First edition, 1998

Library of Congress Cataloging-in-Publication Data
Barasch, Lynne.
     Old friends / Lynne Barasch. — 1st ed.
          p.   cm.
     "Frances Foster books."
     Summary: A very old woman misses all her friends who have died,
especially her best friend, Anna, until she meets a little dog in front of
her apartment.
     ISBN 0-374-35611-4
     [1. Old age—Fiction. 2. Dogs—Fiction.] I. Title.
PZ7.B2296501   1998
[E]—dc21   97-4987

In memory of my grandmother
Helen Kleiner Marx Weiler

Henrietta had lived to a very old age, so old that she had lived longer than all her friends. Being a cheerful woman, Henrietta made the best of it.

She lived on the first floor of a brownstone in the city, where she enjoyed her garden, her books, and her music.

But she was lonely. Most of all, she missed her best friend, Anna, who had died. They had been best friends ever since childhood.

Every morning Henrietta went to the fruit market, and every morning she passed the dog walker waiting in front of her building with several dogs. The dogs always looked bored. But on this morning one little dog seemed very interested in Henrietta and stared.

Henrietta stared back. Then Henrietta thought she heard something.
She thought she heard, "Henrietta, don't you know me?"

Reminding herself that dogs don't talk, Henrietta left quickly for the fruit market, all the while pondering her strange experience with the dog.

"Am I confused?" she thought. "Did I just imagine it? Oh well, I have shopping to do." And she put it out of her mind.

But that night Henrietta had a dream. She dreamed she was a little girl again, playing with Anna. Anna had given her a new china dog for her collection. The china dog looked just like the little dog Henrietta had seen in front of her building that morning.

She woke up with a start. Suddenly Henrietta knew the dog was Anna.
She could hardly wait to find out.

Sure enough, when she went out later that morning, there was the dog
walker with the dogs. The little dog looked at Henrietta. Something in
Henrietta's smile told the little dog that Henrietta understood. Just then
Henrietta heard, "I knew you'd catch on."

Henrietta bent down and hugged her friend. There were tears in her eyes.
"Anna! How I've missed you. I never thought I'd see you again."

The dog walker watched this scene with amusement. Finally she said
to Henrietta, "This little dog has been restless. Now she seems to have
found what she's been looking for. You can take her for her walk if
you'd like. Just bring her back in two hours."

So off to the park they went, Anna and Henrietta.

The way it is with certain friends is how it was with Anna and Henrietta.
An interruption of years seemed like minutes.

They had a lot of catching up to do, but they found in each other the
little girls they had been so long ago.

When they returned home, the dog walker was waiting. It was agreed that Henrietta would take Anna every day. Now life was very full for Henrietta. She was never lonely anymore.

She had only one problem. She couldn't keep up with Anna. Anna wished
Henrietta could run and play and have fun with her the way they used to do.

Henrietta was tired. She felt every bit her age.

In the evenings at home she soaked her feet in hot water and went to bed earlier and earlier.

One night Henrietta had another dream. She was a little girl with Anna
once again. The china dog collection had another new dog in it . . .

one she and Anna had never seen before—a dog with long, dark silky hair, sporting a little red bow.

Next morning the dog walker waited for Henrietta to take Anna as usual,
but she never appeared. The dog walker knocked on Henrietta's door,
but there was no answer.

She left with a sad Anna and the other dogs, wondering where Henrietta was.

She was never to know.

On a fine spring morning, the dog walker came to collect the dogs
as usual. But this morning she had one new dog to collect.

The new dog looked like the china dog in Henrietta's dream, a dog with long, dark silky hair, sporting a little red bow.

Anna, who had been very quiet, was suddenly herself again. She and the
new dog seemed to know each other—

almost as if they were old friends.